Nana's Summer Surprise

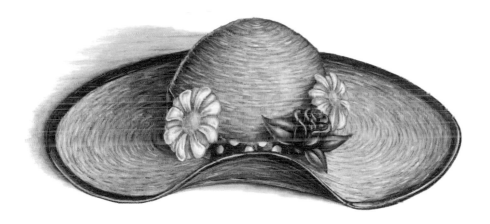

Heather Hartt-Sussman

Illustrated by Georgia Graham

TUNDRA BOOKS

Published in Canada by Tundra Books,
a division of Random House of Canada Limited,
One Toronto Street, Suite 300, Toronto, Ontario M5C 2V6

Published in the United States by Tundra Books of Northern New York,
P.O. Box 1030, Plattsburgh, New York 12901

Library of Congress Control Number: 2012934220

Edited by Sue Tate
Designed by Jennifer Lum
Printed and bound in China

www.tundrabooks.com

Library and Archives Canada Cataloguing in Publication

Hartt-Sussman, Heather
    Nana's summer surprise / Heather Hartt-Sussman ; illustrated
by Georgia Graham.

ISBN 978-1-77049-324-7. – ISBN 978-1-77049-394-0 (EPUB)

    I. Graham, Georgia, 1959- II. Title.

PS8615.A757N37 2013   jC813'.6   C2012-901562-8

We acknowledge the financial support of the Government of Canada
through the Canada Book Fund and that of the Government of Ontario
through the Ontario Media Development Corporation's Ontario Book
Initiative. We further acknowledge the support of the Canada Council for
the Arts and the Ontario Arts Council for our publishing program.

ONTARIO ARTS COUNCIL
CONSEIL DES ARTS DE L'ONTARIO

The artwork in this book was rendered in chalk pastels and chalk pastel pencils
on sanded paper and on cold press illustration board.

1 2 3 4 5 6 18 17 16 15 14 13

For Kathy Lowinger, for believing in Nana.
And for Sue Tate and Georgia Graham,
for helping me bring her to life.
H.H.S.

For my dad, for building our cabin at Gull Lake,
Alberta, and for all of our happy times there.
G.G.

Everything changed the day Nana and Gramps told me that Hortense was coming to stay for the summer.

At first I didn't mind. "Maybe we can go on hikes in the woods, or swing on the tire Gramps tied to the oak tree," I tell Nana.

"Maybe the two of you can even sleep in the tent out back one night," Nana says.

But when her bus arrives, Hortense has changed. She must have grown a full foot taller. She looks like an Amazon, like a giant –

like an adult!

My parents seem thrilled to see her. Everyone grabs her suitcases. Mom hands her a cold bottle of water, telling her how good she looks, despite the long ride.

"I can't get over how you've grown!" says Nana.

"A real young lady," says Gramps, smiling.

I don't think it's all that wonderful. I think Hortense's clothes make her look like a cheerleader or a rock star wannabe. You can't climb trees in a dumb skirt and fancy flip-flops! The thought of her swinging on the tire in that getup makes me kind of giggle.

"Hortense sure has blossomed into a striking young lady," says Nana. And they all walk on ahead of me, talking about Hortense's amazing growth spurt.

"Gross," I say.

When we arrive at the lake house, Hortense gets the bigger bedroom all to herself.

"I thought we were bunking together!" I complain.

"That's not appropriate now," says Gramps.

"You can sleep in here," says Nana, showing me to a room the size of a closet.

I, for one, **am not impressed.**

Later, when Hortense is busy blow-drying her hair, I tell Nana and Gramps my worries.

"There goes the summer," I begin. "Hortense doesn't look like she'll even *want* to play with me anymore."

"You never know," says Nana.

"We have nothing in common now," I complain.

"I bet you can find something, if you try," says Gramps.

I wrack my brain. *What would a young lady, who used to be a girl, like to do all day?* I wonder. *Read fashion magazines? Look at herself in the mirror? Sunbathe?*

"Gross, gross, gross!" I scream.

"You've grown a bit, too, since the last time we saw Hortense," says Nana. "You haven't even given her a chance."

Yeah, but I haven't grown a hundred feet!

"You know," says Gramps, "everyone changes. One day, you are going to have a growth spurt of your own."

Yeah, but I won't forget who I am and become all boring and adult-like and everything!

Nana and Gramps know

I am **not** impressed.

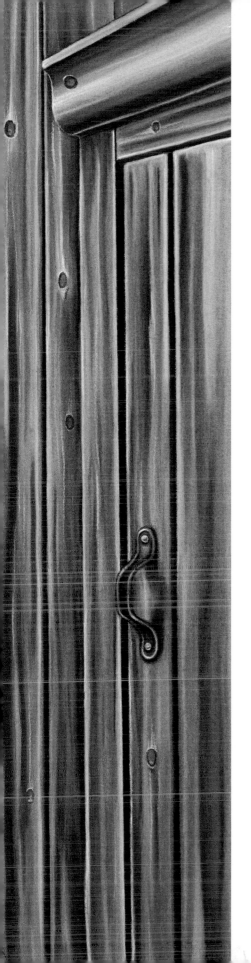

In July, I try everything – I ask Hortense to go berry-picking one day and to build sandcastles the next. I even try acting all mature, and Hortense only laughs!

Sometimes I am so angry that I choose to have dinner in my closet! And Nana, Gramps, and Hortense sit around the table eating, with their shiny silverware and napkins on their laps, like she's one of them. Nana and Gramps might be taken in by the new Hortense.

But I, for one, am not impressed.

By August, I am fed up.

"Hortense seems to be having a wonderful time," says Mom.

"That's just great," I say.

"Her social skills have really improved," says Dad.

"Gross," I say.

Mom and Dad think it's sweet when Hortense hangs posters of movie stars on her bedroom wall. They think it's funny when she tells them all about the boy she has a crush on at school. They think it's cute when she paints her toenails green!

"Kids grow up so quickly," they say.

I, for one, am still not impressed.

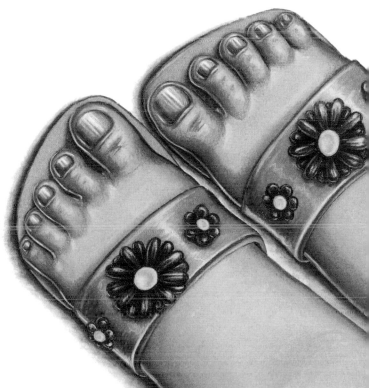

One morning, after she's finished her workout, Hortense comes over and sits me down.

"I know I haven't been playing with you as much as you'd hoped," she says. "And I'm sorry. But I have an idea. It's Nana's birthday at the end of the month. How about we throw her a party?"

"A party would be fun,"
I say. "But it would be **MORE**
fun if it's a surprise!"

"We could do a makeover birthday," suggests Hortense. "Or an all-pink Barbie party. Or how about a Hollywood glamour party, where everyone comes in their fanciest clothes?"

"Gross," I say. This girlie stuff is giving me a headache. "What about a picnic, with all her friends, party hats, and a cake? Nana loves picnics!"

And Hortense agrees.

We do everything to plan the surprise ourselves – write up a guest list, pick a time for the party, make invitations, and choose a cake recipe out of one of Nana's cookbooks.

And, before you know it, Hortense and I are getting along great.

When Nana seems suspicious, we decide to enlist Gramps. So I whisper our plan in his ear.

"Can you keep a secret?" asks Hortense.

"Scout's honor," says Gramps.

"Can you keep a straight face?" I giggle.

"Not sure," he admits, with a chuckle.

In the morning, Nana asks Hortense and me to get up early to watch the fog burn off the lake. We moan and groan and say we want to sleep in, even though we'd already been up making secret plans. When Nana wants to race us across the lake, we say we are too full from breakfast. And when she wants us to dance in the rain in our bathing suits, we pretend we don't think that's fun anymore.

Nana seems hurt, but Gramps comes along to change the subject. "Did you see that bald eagle on the branch out back?" he asks, escorting Nana to the porch. "Come on, dear, I'll race you," he says.

Gramps is a great decoy.

Hortense and I are kind of impressed.

When the big day is finally here, Gramps takes Nana into town. Soon the guests begin to arrive – first Hortense's parents, then the neighbors, then all of Nana's friends.

We spread out all the food that people have brought onto Nana's big picnic blanket. When we hear the van pull up, everyone runs and hides.

"Children, where are you?" cries Nana, coming through the house and out the back door. She's wearing a pretty garden hat that Gramps cleverly bought her in town.

"SURPRISE!"
we all shout, leaping from our hiding spots.

"Happy Birthday, Nana!"

Nana is overjoyed. Her cheeks blush pink. Hortense, Gramps, and I squeeze her tight. We eat our beautiful meal outside, with tea and cake for dessert.

"You look happy, Nana," I say.

"Never happier, my love," she replies. "And just look at that,"
Nana continues, staring me straight in the eye, "I think you've changed
this summer. I could swear that you've actually grown a full foot!"
I give Nana a great big hug. Some things, you never outgrow.

Later it begins to cloud over. We all get into our bathing suits and dance in the rain.